Naughty Fairies

D0306256

WIN A NAUGHTY FAIRIES T-SHIRT!

Every time those Naughty Fairies
are hatching a plan they do their fairy code
where they come up with NF words...

Niggle Flaptart
Nicely Framed
Nimble Fingers

Can you help the Naughty Fairies
find two more words beginning with
N.................. and F....................?

Each month we will select the best entries to win a very
special Naughty Fairies T-shirt and they will go into the
draw to have their NF idea printed in the next lot of books!

Don't forget to include your name and address.
Send your entry to: Naughty Fairies NF Competition,
Hodder Children's Marketing, 338 Euston Road,
London NW1 3BH.
Australian readers should write to:
Hachette Children's Books, Level 17/207 Kent Street,
Sydney, NSW 2000

Collect all the Naughty Fairies books:

Spider
Insider

Lucy Mayflower

*Hodder
Children's
Books*

A division of Hachette Children's Books

Special thanks to Lucy Courtenay

Created by Hodder Children's Books and Lucy Courtenay
Text and illustrations copyright © 2007 Hodder Children's Books
Illustrations created by Artful Doodlers

First published in Great Britain in 2007
by Hodder Children's Books

1

A Catalogue record for this book is available from the British Library

ISBN – 10: 0 340 94433 21
ISBN – 13: 978 0 340 94433 2

Printed in the UK by Bookmarque, Croydon, CR0 4TD

The paper and board used in this paperback by Hodder Children's Books
are natural recyclable products made from wood grown in
sustainable forests. The manufacturing processes conform to the
environmental regulations of the country of origin.

Hodder Children's Books
A division of Hachette Children's Books
338 Euston Rd, London NW1 3BH

Contents

Ambrosia Academy

WOOD STUMP

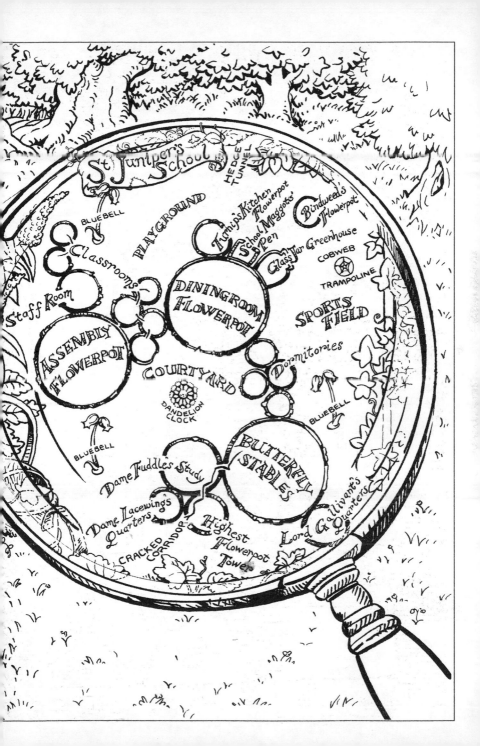

1

A New Subject

Down at the bottom of the garden, something small and red and wriggly flew through the air and landed in a sticky cobweb.

"Good shot, Brilliance," said a slender blonde fairy with a dirty chin.

"It was a *brilliant* shot, Nettle," Brilliance corrected, tucking her wild black hair behind her ears.

Nettle hooked two tiny spider earrings into her ears. "Whatever you say, Champ," she grinned.

"I'm not sure the mites are enjoying this," said an anxious-looking fairy with a thick plait down her back.

"They love it, Sesame," Brilliance

reassured her. The mite in Brilliance's hand gave a high-pitched giggle and waggled its short legs in anticipation.

"Mine's cute," murmured a red-haired fairy in a tattered black and yellow bumblewool dress.

"Don't say that too loudly, Kelpie," warned the smallest fairy, peeling mites off the cobweb target and putting them back in the basket at Brilliance's feet. "Flea might get jealous."

The hairy bumblebee snoozing underneath the cobweb target gave a loud snore.

"Flea?" said Kelpie. "He's never been jealous in his life, Tiptoe. He knows I'll always love him best of all."

"Pong hates it when I talk to the butterflies in the Butterfly Stables," said a spiky-haired fairy.

"That's the difference between bumblebees and dragonflies, Ping," said Kelpie.

"That plus wing size, flight speed and general hovering ability," Ping shot back.

"Excuse me?" said Brilliance loudly. "I was halfway through my go."

"We aren't stopping you," said Kelpie.

Brilliance aimed at the cobweb target.

"Brilliance?" said Tiptoe.

"Hmm?" said Brilliance, turning her

head and letting go of the mite at the same time.

The mite missed the target and sailed through a narrow flowerpot window nearby. There was a splash and a squeal. The flowerpot door flew open and a tall, wet-looking teacher glared out at the Naughty Fairies.

"Mite darts are forbidden in the courtyard," said Dame Lacewing in a voice that could freeze bird feet to twigs. She held the bedraggled mite between two long fingers. "This creature is lucky that my chicory coffee had cooled down."

"Sorry, Dame Lacewing," chorused the Naughty Fairies.

"Can I have my mite back, please?" Brilliance asked.

"No," said Dame Lacewing. "You should be in the Assembly Flowerpot by now. Didn't you hear Dame Fuddle's announcement at breakfast? Hurry up

or you're going to be late."

"What were you going to say anyway, Tiptoe?" asked Brilliance, as they trailed after Dame Lacewing across the courtyard of the famous St Juniper's School for Fairies.

"That we were going to be late for

Dame Fuddle's assembly," said Tiptoe.

"So you *did* listen at breakfast?" said Sesame looking impressed.

Tiptoe nodded.

"What's the assembly about, then?" asked Nettle.

"The SPARCLE report," said Tiptoe. "It came by pixie post this morning."

"But we passed the SPARCLE inspection," objected Ping, as they found a space on the beaten earth floor of the Assembly Flowerpot among the other fairies of St Juniper's. "The SPARCLE school inspectors came on Kelpie's flutterday, remember?"

"This is the full report," said Tiptoe. "There's going to be some kind of change, Dame Fuddle said."

Before the other Naughty Fairies could ask Tiptoe for more information, a large fairy bounced on to the half-brick stage and waved her wand for her pupils' attention.

"Good morning!" beamed Dame
Fuddle. The Head of St Juniper's was
fond of exclamation marks. "Thank you
for arriving so promptly! Quieten down
now, dears!"

"What is Dame Fuddle *wearing?*" said
Ping, as the noise in the flowerpot got
steadily louder.

"I think it's a poppy," said Sesame.

"A poppy that has been eaten by a
slug and sicked up again," said Kelpie.

Dame Fuddle hopelessly waved her
wand for silence. As the fairies
chattered on, a large bearded pixie in a
pink petal apron climbed on to the
stage with a snort.

"Shut up, ye winged wombats!"
roared the pixie.

Turnip was the school cook. He kept
handfuls of pignuts in his apron
pockets, and threw them at fairies who
annoyed him. No one wanted a pignut
in the ear, so the flowerpot fell quiet.

"Before Dame Fuddle begins, I want a word," said Turnip, planting his large feet on the stage. "As fire warden of St Juniper's, I advise ye to attend tonight's fire practice. Getting burnt to a crisp will be nothing compared to a detention with me and the rest of these pignuts. That's it."

"Thank you, Turnip!" said Dame Fuddle, hauling up the lower half of her poppy outfit, which looked in danger of falling down. "Now, on with our assembly! On SPARCLE's recommendation, we are introducing a new school subject!"

"Snail racing!" called a fairy in the front row.

Other suggestions followed, including slug boiling and beetle polishing.

"The new subject," announced Dame Fuddle, "will be dressmaking!"

There was a gasp of horror.

"Knitting bumblewool and making the

basics is one thing," said Kelpie in disgust. "But *dressmaking?* Patterns and *fashion?* That's what *pink* fairies do."

"Like the fairies at *Ambrosia Academy*," Nettle groaned.

"I love wearing pink," said Brilliance in a simpering Ambrosia Academy fairy voice.

"Pansy pants!" sniggered Sesame.

Tiptoe giggled. "Floaty frocks! Ha-ha-hyacinth hats!"

The Naughty Fairies exploded with laughter.

"Our dear butterfly-riding teacher, Lord Gallivant, has agreed to take the dressmaking class!" Dame Fuddle continued, raising her voice over the noise in the Assembly Flowerpot. "Lord Gallivant? Over to you!"

A handsome elf in a shiny ivy-leaf suit stood up and bowed graciously to the assembled fairies. "I prefer to call it fairytailoring, Dame Fuddle," he said, twinkling at the Head Teacher.

This made the Naughty Fairies laugh even more.

"Fairytailoring," said Lord Gallivant with great dignity, "is a fine fairy tradition. You will learn to make dresses and hats and shoes. When I won the Midsummer Champion Butterfly Race—"

The listening fairies groaned. Lord Gallivant never tired of telling his pupils about his triumph at the Midsummer Champion Butterfly Race.

"When I won the Midsummer Champion Butterfly Race," Lord Gallivant repeated loudly, "I designed my own racing outfit. The judges agreed that there had never been a better-dressed Champion." He twitched the lapels of his suit. "I will share my secrets with you," he continued, "and we will show Ambrosia Academy that St Juniper's fairies are not a bunch of winged bumpkins who can't tell the difference between a slipstitch and a sausage!"

"A slip what?" Sesame said.

"A sausage?" Tiptoe said.

"What's Ambrosia Academy got to do with it?" asked Brilliance.

"There will also be a new inter-school event in the school calendar!" Dame Fuddle announced as Lord Gallivant sat down again. "The Fairy Fashion Show! There will be five categories, and so five outfits, from each school, to be judged by none other than the Fairy Queen herself!"

The Assembly Flowerpot fell silent at the mention of the fearsomely fashionable Fairy Queen.

"The Show will take place in four weeks' time!" continued Dame Fuddle. Her exclamation marks were getting louder with every sentence. "St Juniper's and Ambrosia Academy will battle to win the prestigious Fashion

Feather for the best design! We shall all learn something new and have lots of fun!" Dame Fuddle hauled up her poppy outfit again. "Assembly dismissed!" she twittered, and bounced off the stage.

"What planet is Dame Fuddle on?" said Ping, as the Naughty Fairies barged out of the flowerpot and into the sunshine again. "When has St Juniper's ever had fun with the fairies of Ambrosia Academy?"

"I'd rather wedge stinging nettles up my nose," said Kelpie.

"We have to win the Fashion Feather for St Juniper's," Brilliance announced.

"But that means we'll have to listen during fairytailoring lessons," said Tiptoe in dismay.

"And do homework," Sesame said.

"And *sew*," said Kelpie

Brilliance fluttered her wings crossly. "Do you want Ambrosia Academy to win?" she demanded. "Operation

Fashion Feather begins as soon as we start fairytailoring with Lord Gallivant. Agreed?"

2

Fairytailoring

Lord Gallivant had turned the empty
flowerpot at the top of St Juniper's
highest flowerpot tower into his new
Fairytailoring classroom.

There were piles of petals all over the
floor. Red ones, yellow ones, delicate
blue ones and crazy purple ones. There
were pots of splinter needles, shell
scissors and prickle pins on the fairies'
new desks. Two money spiders were
spinning silk in one corner. In another
corner stood a peculiar beeswax figure
that vaguely resembled a fairy.

"What's this?" said Nettle, going up
to the figure and poking it.

"That," said Lord Gallivant, "is

Wanda. She's our fairytailoring dummy."

"She does look pretty stupid," said
Brilliance as the fairies sat down.

"Our *modelling* dummy, Brilliance,"
Lord Gallivant said.

"What's under that moss blanket,
Lord Gallivant?" asked Sesame.

Lord Gallivant stepped up to the moss
blanket on the floor and pulled it away

with a flourish. A very fat white grub peered out of a grass-weave cage at the class.

"*Bombyx mori*," said Lord Gallivant. "The silkworm. Obtained at great expense, I might add."

"Ahhh!" Sesame breathed.

"Gross," said Ping.

"It looks like an overfed maggot," said Brilliance.

"Give me a bee any day," Kelpie agreed, stroking Flea.

"We shall be studying our silkworm in detail," said Lord Gallivant. "It should pupate and produce some silk in time for the Fairy Fashion Show."

"Let's call him Dollop," suggested Sesame, reaching into the cage to tickle the grub under the chin. "Because he's so squashy."

Dollop tucked his nose underneath his plump white belly and started snoring.

"We have just four weeks before the Fairy Fashion Show," said Lord Gallivant. "Four weeks to cut a petal so that a skirt falls *just so*. Four weeks to design five fabulous garments to win the Fashion Feather for St Juniper's."

"Four weeks to sock it to Ambrosia Academy," added Nettle.

The other fairies in the Fairytailoring class cheered.

"Choose a petal, collect a twist of
spider silk, and return to your desks,"
Lord Gallivant instructed. "Today, we
shall make hats."

"Hats?" complained Brilliance. "The
Fashion Feather won't be awarded for a
stupid *hat*."

Lord Gallivant wagged a finger at her.
"Accessories are essential, Brilliance.
And one cannot fly before one can
walk," he said. "One must always start
with something small."

"Like Lord Gallivant's brain," Kelpie
whispered to Ping.

Soon the classroom was full of busy
fairies. Petal snippets floated through
the air, making Flea sneeze. Lord
Gallivant had already made an
enormous hat out of a bluebell, and was
modelling it around the flowerpot,
showing fairies the tiny stitches in the
pale blue brim.

"Lord Gallivant is loving this," said

Ping, trying to bend a stiff rose petal
into shape. "Ow!" she added crossly as
the rose petal flicked back and whacked
her on the nose.

"What *are* you making, Kelpie?"
asked Brilliance, peering at the
enormous grass and primrose-petal
creation in Kelpie's lap. "A suitcase?"

"I figured the bigger the better," said
Kelpie. She tucked a stray piece of

grass into the brim of her hat and admired the result. "A really huge hat is sure to catch Lord Gallivant's eye."

"Ouch," said Ping as her rose petal flicked out of place again.

"Ping's hat might catch Lord Gallivant's eye as well," said Nettle. "But not in a good way."

Fairies ran up and down the classroom, trying their hats on Wanda the wax fairy. The flowerpot was starting to look like a summer meadow as more and more petal fragments floated to the floor.

"Five more dandelion seeds!" announced Lord Gallivant.

"Finished," announced Kelpie to the other Naughty Fairies.

She picked up her enormous hat and placed it on her head. It immediately fell over her eyes.

With a shrill bee-squeal of terror, Flea leaped into the air. He ricocheted

around the room and disappeared at
full speed through the window.

"I don't think Flea really likes hats,"
said Sesame.

After supper, the Naughty Fairies
headed off to find some flax in the
Hedge Tunnel.

"The Fairy Queen's dresses are
always sewn with flax," Brilliance said.

"And if it's good enough for the Fairy Queen, it's good enough for us."

"We'd better win this Fashion Feather," Ping grumbled. "I wanted to ride my dragonfly tonight."

"What's that noise?"" Kelpie asked, peering among the brambles and the elderberries of the Hedge.

The Naughty Fairies cocked their heads. There was a faint buzzing sound up ahead. They flew into the tunnel and headed for the noise.

Halfway along the tunnel, Nettle suddenly stopped and hissed: *"Ambrosia Academy!"*

Through a tangle of hazel twigs, the Naughty Fairies saw three Ambrosia Academy fairies with a large cricket on a grass leash.

"Start sawing, cricket," ordered the prettiest Ambrosia fairy. She gave the cricket a push.

The cricket started buzzing its back

leg against the stem of a tall, pale blue
flower. It was the buzzing sound the
Naughty Fairies had been following.

"This stem should give us enough flax
to stitch our outfits for the Fairy Fashion
Show," the prettiest fairy was saying to
her friends. "Mummy says it's much
stronger than spider silk."

The cricket stopped buzzing its back
leg. The pale blue flower toppled over.

"Pick it up," the pretty fairy ordered her friends.

"But Glitter," moaned the taller of the other two fairies. "It's all sticky!"

"Just *pick it up*," Glitter snarled.

The hazel stem Tiptoe was leaning against suddenly snapped. To the Naughty Fairies' horror, Tiptoe rolled out of her hiding place and came to a stop at Glitter's feet.

"Well well well," Glitter purred,

staring down at Tiptoe. "A little Juniper caterpillar."

"Who are you calling a caterpillar?" Kelpie demanded, stepping out of the undergrowth.

Tiptoe struggled to her feet as the other Naughty Fairies joined Kelpie. Glitter dropped the cricket's leash and backed nervously towards her friends.

"You're outnumbered," said Nettle, as the cricket took his chance and hopped off at speed.

"I would advise you and your little pink friends to beat it," added Ping.

"Thanks for the flax," said Brilliance, giving Glitter her most brilliant smile. "We'll use it in the Fairy Fashion Show, I think."

"You'll need more than flax to win the Fashion Feather," snarled Glitter.

"We've got it sewn up already," said Kelpie. "If you'll pardon the pun."

"*You?*" Glitter giggled. "Win the

Feather? You've only got to look at your Head Teacher to see that St Juniper's has *zero* style."

"Dame Fuddle will make your Head Teacher look like a soggy slug at the Fashion Show!" Tiptoe said bravely. "Just see if she doesn't."

This made the Ambrosia Academy fairies laugh even harder.

"If you can make Dame Fuddle look better than Lady Campion at the Fairy Fashion Show," giggled Glitter, "then I'll dance naked around the Wood Stump."

"You'd better hope it's a warm night!" Tiptoe shouted as Glitter and her two friends turned around and flounced off into the Hedge.

"So had you!" Glitter shot back over her shoulder. "Because when the Fairy Queen says that Lady Campion's outfit is better than Dame Fuddle's, you'll be the ones doing the dancing!"

And still laughing, the Ambrosia fairies flew away.

3

Fire!

"Tiptoe?" said Brilliance when the Ambrosia Academy fairies had gone.

"Yes?" said Tiptoe.

"There's no way Dame Fuddle will beat Lady Campion at the Fashion Show!" Brilliance hissed. "Have you forgotten that poppy outfit? Lady Campion wears *lilies*!"

"And the Fairy Queen is the judge, for Nature's sake!" said Ping. "She's only the most fashionable fairy in the whole fairy world!"

"Looks like we'll be the ones dancing round the Wood Stump after all," said Sesame gloomily.

"And that is *so* not brilliant," said

Brilliance, looking thunderous.

"Who says we can't make over Dame Fuddle?" said Tiptoe.

Kelpie shook her head. "Impossible."

"Naughty Fairies!" challenged Tiptoe. She stuck out her fist and waited for the others to do their fairy code.

"Not funny," muttered Nettle at last, putting her fist on Tiptoe's.

"Never fashionable," added Ping with a sigh.

"Nasty frills," Kelpie said, shuddering.

"Gnarled ferret," said Sesame, getting her spelling wrong as usual.

Brilliance put her fist on the pile last of all. "Nitwit fairy," she growled.

"Fly, fly . . . to the SKY!"

The Naughty Fairies flung their hands into the air.

"We've got four weeks to get this right," said Tiptoe. "We've already got flax for sewing. Now we need to find out about the best fabrics and the most fashionable designs. We then make our dress, and persuade Dame Fuddle to wear it."

"Not much to do, then," said Ping sarcastically.

"I still say it's impossible," declared Kelpie.

"Well, we've all NFed now," said Tiptoe firmly. "So we've got to *un*impossible it. Right?"

The Naughty Fairies stashed the flax stem in the Fairytailoring class, ready for the next lesson. Back out in the courtyard, the first person they saw was Dame Fuddle herself.

"You look nice today, Dame Fuddle," said Nettle.

Dame Fuddle looked down at her wonky brown leaf trousers, which clashed horribly with her knitted moss cardigan. "Do you think so, Nettle dear?" she said. "That's very kind of you to say so!"

"You've got a real eye for fashion, Dame Fuddle," continued Brilliance.

"You're an inspiration," added Sesame breathily.

"In fact," said Tiptoe, "we'd love to design a dress for the evening-wear category, for you to wear at the Fairy Fashion Show."

"Don't worry about dressing little old me!" Dame Fuddle said, flapping her hands coyly. "My trusty marigold jumpsuit will do for the Fairy Fashion Show! It's seen me through plenty of fashionable occasions and hasn't let me down yet!"

"Her marigold jumpsuit?" Ping asked as Dame Fuddle continued across the courtyard. "Isn't that, like – orange?"

"Yup," said Kelpie.

"With brown and yellow and red stripes," said Sesame.

"And a frilly bit of green leaf around the neck," said Nettle.

"Totally wrong for her complexion," Brilliance said.

"Ew," said Ping faintly.

"We have to get rid of that suit," said Tiptoe. "Then Dame Fuddle will have to wear whatever we make. Does anyone know a spell?"

"Who needs a spell?" said Kelpie. And winked.

Twenty dandelion seeds later, the Naughty Fairies were hiding underneath the window sill of Dame Fuddle's study. The sun was setting and heavy shadows fell across the courtyard.

Brilliance peered over the ledge. The study was dark.

"Hand it over, Kelpie," she whispered.

Kelpie opened the leaf box she was carrying and pulled out a sleepy firefly.

"This is a bit drastic," said Tiptoe

nervously, as Brilliance dropped the firefly over the window ledge and shooed it towards Dame Fuddle's twiggy clothes rail.

"You're the one who suggested it," said Kelpie.

"I didn't suggest burning all of Dame Fuddle's clothes with a firefly," Tiptoe objected.

The Naughty Fairies watched as the firefly shuffled towards the clothes rail. Its tail was beginning to look red hot.

"It's the most brilliant suggestion I've ever heard," said Brilliance. "We can get rid of everything now."

"The poppy suit," said Nettle.

"Those green sweet-wrapper dungarees," said Ping.

"That really horrible daffodil gown Dame Fuddle wore to the Bluebell Ball," said Kelpie.

"What's not to celebrate?" said Sesame.

The trailing hem of a bright purple iris

cloak with caterpillar holes all over it began to smoulder. Half in terror and half in delight, the Naughty Fairies watched as flames began to lick up the clothes rail and smoke twisted through the air.

Overhead, a snowbell began to clang furiously.

"The fire alarm!" squeaked Tiptoe.

Doors and windows flew open all over St Juniper's.

"Fire!"

"Dame Fuddle's study!"

"Make way for the fire warden! *Make way!*"

The Naughty Fairies flattened themselves into the shadows as Turnip came galloping around the corner with a small grasshopper on a grass leash.

"Niblick!" Turnip roared. "In there, ye great leaping lug!"

The little grasshopper dashed through the door to Dame Fuddle's study.

"And – *widdle!*" Turnip bellowed.

Niblick lifted his leg and widdled smartly on the flames. There was a hiss and a squeak of outrage from the firefly, and the fire was out.

Turnip turned very slowly to face the Naughty Fairies.

"Well done, Turnip," said Brilliance.

"That fire came out of nowhere," Ping said innocently.

"I was about to ring the snowbell myself," Tiptoe said.

"Only she wasn't tall enough," Sesame added.

The Naughty Fairies prayed that

Turnip hadn't seen them put the firefly
through Dame Fuddle's window.

"Aye, well," grunted Turnip. "No harm
done I suppose."

"Worse luck," Kelpie muttered in a
low voice to Nettle.

Turnip took a pignut from his apron
pocket and tossed it up and down in his
beefy hand. The Naughty Fairies eyed

the pignut nervously.

"I didn't see ye at the fire practice this evening," said Turnip.

"No, Turnip," squeaked Ping.

"Sorry, Turnip," Nettle said.

To their relief, Turnip put his pignut away and patted his pocket.

"A wee bit of honesty does wonders for my mood," said the cook. "Detention tomorrow morning at sunrise for the lot of ye in Lord Gallivant's classroom. And *don't* be late."

4

Wolf Spiders

At sunrise the following morning, the Naughty Fairies arrived in the Fairytailoring classroom for their detention. Turnip had pinned their instructions on to Wanda the wax fairy.

"You have half a dandelion to complete this task," Sesame read. "Or you will miss the ants' egg omelettes at breakfast. Happy shovelling. Turnip."

The Naughty Fairies stared at the six hazelnut-shell shovels lined up against Lord Gallivant's desk. Dollop the silkworm blinked at them.

"It could have been worse," said Brilliance at last.

"What's worse than shovelling

silkworm poo?" grumbled Kelpie.

"Better get on with it," said Tiptoe.
"I haven't had an ants' egg omelette
in ages."

Dollop inched out of his cage and
curled up underneath Lord Gallivant's
desk as the fairies sighed and rolled up
their sleeves.

Cleaning out Dollop's cage was hot,
smelly work. The Naughty Fairies
shovelled and argued, argued some
more and shovelled some more. No one
could think of how they were going to
make Dame Fuddle wear their Fairy
Fashion Show creation.

"If only our fire plan had worked,"
grumbled Brilliance.

"Persuading Dame Fuddle to wear
something is the least of our problems,"
Kelpie pointed out. "We've got to make
the thing first."

"Lord Gallivant's got a great library of
books on fairytailoring," said Nettle,

resting her hand on her shovel and
staring up at the bookshelves. "*A
Beginners' Guide to Fairy Fashion. Petal
Patterns. Witchy Stitches.*"

"Anything on the best materials for
evening wear?" asked Tiptoe.

"How about this?" Nettle asked. She
passed a book bound in tattered
cobwebs to Brilliance.

"*Sew Silky,*" Kelpie read, peering over
Brilliance's shoulder.

"It looks perfect," said Ping.

"Why am I the only one still shovelling?" Sesame complained as the others put the book on Lord Gallivant's desk and started flicking eagerly through the pages.

"Someone has to," said Kelpie. "Or Turnip will kill us."

"And Tiptoe won't get her omelette," Nettle added.

Grumbling, Sesame returned to cleaning out the silkworm's cage as Brilliance read a passage out loud from *Sew Silky*.

"Wolf spiders produce the highest quality spider silk, much sought after by fairytailors. Its stretchy qualities make it perfect for the fuller fairy figure. It blends very well with cornflowers."

"We've got flax, and cornflowers really suit Dame Fuddle," said Tiptoe in excitement. "If we can find wolf spider silk, we'll make a dress that will blow the Fairy Queen's crown off! There's bound to be wolf spiders in the Wood."

"We'll go and look for wolf spiders this afternoon," Brilliance decided. "How's the shovelling going, Sesame?"

"It's finally done," said Sesame, wiping her face. "But you all owe me a honeycake."

"Pooh," said Nettle, wrinkling her nose and staring at the snoozing silkworm. "I think Dollop just farted."

"Better get him back in his cage before he gives us something else to shovel," Kelpie advised.

That afternoon, the Naughty Fairies ate a quick lunch of elderberry fritters washed down with clover juice and hurried over to the Butterfly Stables to fetch Pong, Ping's dragonfly. Pong was long, slim and bad-tempered, and fitted the six Naughty Fairies on his back very neatly.

"It's all very well saying there's wolf spiders in the Wood," said Kelpie as Ping guided Pong over the Hedge and across the Meadow. "But *where* in the Wood?"

"We'll start on the edge of the Wood and work inwards," said Brilliance. "We'll find wolf spiders sooner or later."

The tiny spiders in Nettle's ears shivered and hid behind her earlobes.

"I've got a nasty feeling about this," Nettle said.

Ping brought Pong down to land at the base of a beech tree on the edge of the Wood.

"We'll go that way," said Brilliance, pointing. "It's dark and scary-looking. Spiders always live in dark and scary-looking places."

Following close behind Brilliance, the Naughty Fairies flew silently through the trees. The woodland air felt damp on their wings, and the sun seemed very far away.

Deep in the darkest and scariest part
of the Wood, Brilliance landed on a
hazel leaf and folded away her wings.

"This is horrible," moaned Sesame as
she swooped in beside Kelpie. Ping
followed close behind.

"Let's not be too long," suggested
Nettle, landing beside Brilliance. "My

ear spiders are hiding so far down my ears that they're practically coming out of my nose."

Tiptoe suddenly came in to land much too fast. She crashed into Nettle, who bumped into Brilliance, who knocked over Sesame, who collided with both Kelpie and Ping – and six Naughty Fairies fell backwards off the hazel leaf. Before they could unfurl their wings, they had crashed on to the ground.

They lay on the forest floor and

blinked up at the sky.

"Is it night time?" asked Kelpie groggily. "I can see stars."

"Sorry," Tiptoe panted.

"I can't move my wings," complained Ping in an anxious voice.

"Me neither," Brilliance said. "They're stuck to something."

Sesame peered over her shoulder. "It's a web," she said.

"If this is the web," said Ping, "then where's the spider?"

Nettle's ear spiders wailed.

"Remember that nasty feeling I mentioned a while back?" said Nettle.

The Naughty Fairies tried not to think about the spider that might or might not be about to eat them.

"We need a brilliant plan," said Brilliance.

"And you've got one?" said Nettle.

"No," Brilliance replied.

"How about we all hold hands?" suggested Tiptoe. "We can pull together on the count of three."

"That's the stupidest plan I've ever heard," Brilliance said.

"I think the spider's coming," said Kelpie.

The web shivered. Turning their heads, the fairies saw a hairy-legged spider

with gleaming eyes staring at them with interest.

"It's a wolf spider," Nettle squeaked. "I recognise the eyes from that picture in Lord Gallivant's book!"

"Hold hands," Brilliance said rather quickly. "One, two, three – PULL!"

The Naughty Fairies heaved hard.

With a sticky, tearing sound, the web broke and they were free.

"*I* had a brilliant plan!" said Tiptoe in excitement, as the Naughty Fairies soared up and away from the web, still trailing glistening spider threads. "*Me!*"

"Yada yada yada," said Brilliance.

"That was close," said Kelpie, breathing hard.

"We got a bit of wolf-spider silk," said Nettle, peering over her shoulder at her wings. "It's stuck all over us."

"But it's not enough," Ping said. "Is it, Brilliance?"

"No," said Brilliance. "We have to go back down there to get some more."

The afternoon sun was almost gone. The moon was rising now, and all around there were strange sounds as the night creatures of the Wood began to stir.

"What's that noise?"asked Tiptoe nervously.

and dangled in a dead faint from her
earlobes.

"More wolf spiders!" said Nettle.

"They look quite sweet really," said
Sesame doubtfully.

"If you like hairy spiders with shiny
eyes," Ping said.

"What are they doing?" Tiptoe asked.

"I think they're singing," said
Brilliance in disbelief.

"Catchy," said Kelpie. "Not."

The wolf spiders were drumming their
feet again. They bowed their furry
heads and wagged their furry bottoms,
and all the time their eyes shone like
tiny fireflies in the gloom.

The Naughty Fairies noticed that the
spider in the web had scuttled out to
join her friends. There was a cocoon of
silk attached to her spinners.

"Just one of those would be enough
for Dame Fuddle's dress," said Tiptoe.

"So who's going to get it?" Nettle asked.

The Naughty Fairies could hear a strange drumming sound down on the forest floor. It was getting closer.

Twelve hairy spiders came into view. They were marching in a line, their long, furry legs drumming hard on the ground. Nettle's ear spiders squealed

They all looked at Sesame.

"Why me?" Sesame protested. "It's always me!"

"You like spiders," said Brilliance. "We just need that teensy ball of silk, Sesame. The spider's not even looking this way. You could swoop in and grab it – easy."

The silk cocoon dangled temptingly from the spider's back.

"Go on," Nettle said, giving Sesame a gentle push.

Sesame flew down to the forest floor as quietly as she could. The spiders were still drumming their legs. The others watched from a safe distance as Sesame reached for the silk and unhooked it very carefully from the spider's back.

The drumming stopped. Sesame froze as very slowly, the spiders turned and stared at her.

"Thanks," squeaked Sesame, backing

away. "Great tune, by the way. La la la."

"Go!" screamed Brilliance as the wolf spiders reared up on their hind legs.

The Naughty Fairies darted away from the wolf spiders like arrows with Sesame clinging on to the cocoon for dear life, heading for the edge of the Wood, Pong – and safety!

5

Hot Water

The next three weeks passed in a blur
of fairytailoring as the Fairy Fashion
Show grew closer. The fairies learned
about invisible seams, bodice
embroidery, shell-button carving and
buttonhole making. Slowly, the piles of
petals were transformed into a pretty
array of frocks and frills. Apart from
moulding Wanda the wax fairy into
rude shapes when Lord Gallivant
wasn't looking, the pupils of St
Juniper's had never behaved so well or
worked so hard. It was remarkable what
an inter-school competition could
achieve.

The only problem was Dollop the

silkworm, who was getting fatter and
smellier but showing no sign of
producing any silk.

"I don't understand it," said Lord
Gallivant the day before the Fairy
Fashion Show. "The imp who sold me
this silkworm assured me that it would
pupate within three weeks! Next time I
see him, I shall have words!"

"And those words shall be Midsummer, Champion, Butterfly and Race," Nettle intoned, which made the others giggle.

The Naughty Fairies' evening gown was starting to look wonderful. The seams were tightly sewn with flax, the wolf-spider silk bodice shimmered like water, and the long cornflower skirt was caught up at the front, showing a pale primrose lining sewn by Brilliance and Tiptoe. While Ping and Nettle worked on a pair of jasmine bloomers to go beneath the gown, Sesame and Kelpie embroidered the skirt with tiny ants. Even Kelpie had joined in, stitching a rather wonky bumblebee on to one shoulder.

"I still can't believe how lucky we were to find that wolf spider," said Sesame happily. "We got enough silk to weave the bodice *and* embroider one hundred and twelve ants on Dame Fuddle's gown."

"Plus one bee," Kelpie added.

Brilliance pulled out a string of fluffy white pompoms from underneath the table. "These were right in the middle of the wolf-spider cocoon," she said. "They'll look fantastic sewn around the hem, promise."

Nettle and Ping pinned the pompoms around the hem of the dress and Brilliance and Tiptoe sewed them into place. The pompoms were white and fluffy, and made the gown look like it was edged with snow.

"Not bad," said Nettle. "For a frock."

Sesame put down her shell scissors. "It might look great," she said, "but we still haven't persuaded Dame Fuddle to wear it and the Fairy Fashion Show's tomorrow."

"She hasn't even come to look at it," said Kelpie. "Every time we bring up the subject, she goes on about her marigold jumpsuit."

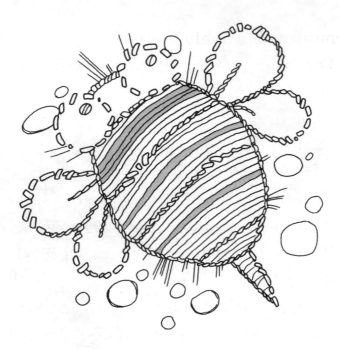

"I can feel Glitter laughing at my bottom already," said Sesame gloomily.

"We could try and burn Dame Fuddle's clothes again," Ping said.

"Why don't we just steal them?" Tiptoe suggested.

"You're getting quite good at brilliant ideas, Tiptoe," said Brilliance in admiration. "We can steal them tonight, when Dame Fuddle's asleep. Then she'll *have* to wear our gown tomorrow. Naughty Fairies!"

The Naughty Fairies quickly piled up their fists.

"Nice frills!"

"Nearly finished!"

"Newly fantastic!"

"Nooble frooble," Sesame said.

"You made that up," Ping accused.

"So?" said Sesame. "It starts with NF, doesn't it?"

"Naked fairies," said Kelpie, putting her hand on the pile last of all. "But not us, with any luck."

"My dears!" gasped Lord Gallivant, rushing up to the Naughty Fairies and pressing his hand to his heart. "This simply *must* be our piece for the evening-wear category. The Fairy Queen will adore it! Who will be modelling it?"

"Dame Fuddle," said Brilliance.

"No teasing now," said Lord Gallivant with a hearty laugh.

"Dame Fuddle," Ping repeated patiently.

Lord Gallivant's face cleared. "I see!" he said. "You're keeping it a secret for tomorrow, eh? Jolly good! Best of luck! I have high hopes of winning that Feather!"

"No," Tiptoe began. "It really is for Dame—"

But Lord Gallivant had already moved on to the next design, a miniskirt that looked like an exploding snowdrop.

"Are we the only ones who think Dame Fuddle's going to wear our dress?" said Sesame in despair.

"Dame Fuddle *will* wear it," Brilliance insisted. "You'll see. Tonight at midnight. Outside Dame Fuddle's flowerpot. This is it, guys. This is our last chance!"

That night, the Naughty Fairies tiptoed across the courtyard to Dame Fuddle's darkened flowerpot.

"Guard the door, Flea," Kelpie whispered. "If Dame Lacewing comes, buzz really loudly."

Very carefully, the Naughty Fairies pushed open the door and peered inside. Dame Fuddle was sleeping peacefully in an enormous pansy nightgown and matching hat, a half-finished cup of hot nettle tea and a box of sugared buttercups by her bedside.

Brilliance reached for the clothes still hanging on the now rather singed twig clothes rail. The Naughty Fairies gathered up old petal frocks, mouldy leaf trousers, the poppy outfit and the sweet-wrapper dungarees. Last of all, Nettle unhooked the orange marigold jumpsuit and draped it carefully over her arm. Then, as quietly as they could, the Naughty Fairies backed out of the flowerpot with their booty.

"I'm almost afraid to ask where you are taking those."

Sesame squealed and dropped the sweet-wrapper dungarees as Dame Lacewing stopped tickling Flea's tummy and stood up.

"How tall you are, Dame Lacewing," said Tiptoe weakly.

"Explain what you are doing with the contents of Dame Fuddle's wardrobe in the middle of the night," said Dame Lacewing in a dangerous voice.

"Um," said Ping. "Laundry?"

The next morning, the Naughty Fairies
found themselves in Dame Lacewing's
study on detention. Two walnut-shell
cauldrons full of hot water were
steaming gently in the middle of the
room, and a pile of pebble-irons stood
heating up beside the fire. Beside the

cauldrons lay the clothes that the Naughty Fairies had tried to steal the night before.

"Laundry time," said Dame Lacewing. She handed the Naughty Fairies a large bunch of soapwort. "I expect this to be washed, dried and ironed by lunchtime. And I'll have your wands," the teacher added, holding out her hand. "There will be no washing spells, no drying spells and certainly no ironing spells. You would probably burn down the entire school."

"But the Fairy Fashion Show is this evening and we've still got loads to do!" Tiptoe wailed.

The Naughty Fairies all began talking at once.

"We've been working on our dress for ages . . ."

"Lord Gallivant wants it for the evening-wear category . . ."

"Wolf-spider silk . . ."

"Pompoms . . ."

"We made it for Dame Fuddle," said Brilliance. "She *has* to wear it at the Show, Dame Lacewing!"

"Why?" Dame Lacewing asked. "Have you lined it with stinging nettles? Have you stitched it together with stinking goosefoot?"

"Come and see it, Dame Lacewing," begged Tiptoe. "Lord Gallivant thinks it could win the Fashion Feather!"

"But we made it for Dame Fuddle," added Kelpie. "It won't fit anyone else."

"And this is why you took Dame Fuddle's clothes?" Dame Lacewing asked. "So that she would wear your dress at the Show?"

The Naughty Fairies nodded.

"Why didn't you just ask her?" said Dame Lacewing.

"We did," Sesame said. "About a million times."

"We really want to win the Fashion

Feather for St Juniper's," said Ping earnestly. "The reputation of our school depends on it."

"And your own reputations as well, no doubt," said Dame Lacewing.

For several extremely long dandelion seeds, the Fairy Maths teacher stared at them. The Naughty Fairies hardly dared to blink.

"I shall probably regret this," said the teacher at last, "but I want you to show me this gown."

"What about Dame Fuddle's laundry?" asked Sesame.

Dame Lacewing flicked her wand at the pile of clothes. *"Lava!"* she said shortly. *"Seca! Passa!"*

The clothes whipped off the floor and plunged themselves into the first cauldron. The soapwort danced out of Nettle's hand and leaped into the cauldron as well. In a swoosh of froth and water, the clothes jumped into the

second cauldron and out again almost
instantly. From the fireplace, several
red-hot pebbles threw themselves at the
clothes and pressed them to perfection.
Last of all, the clothes fell in a neat,
sweet-smelling pile on an acorn chair
by the door.

"Wow," said Nettle.

"Brilliant!" gasped Brilliance.

"I think you shrank the sweet-wrapper dungarees, Dame Lacewing," said Kelpie.

"A tragedy," said Dame Lacewing. "Now take me to this frock."

"Lavender!" called Dame Fuddle, hurrying towards Dame Lacewing and the Naughty Fairies as they crossed the courtyard towards the Fairytailoring classroom. She was still wearing her pansy nightgown and cap. "The most extraordinary thing has happened! All my clothes have disappeared! Simply vanished! I can't understand it!"

"It is all in hand, Fenella," said Dame Lacewing without breaking her stride. "Come with us now. Brilliance and her friends have something they wish to show you."

6

Showtime

The Naughty Fairies followed Dame
Fuddle and Dame Lacewing up to the
Fairytailoring classroom.

"I haven't been this nervous since I
threw an apple pip at Nettle and it hit
Turnip," said Kelpie.

"What if Dame Fuddle doesn't like
it?" Ping asked.

"I can feel the evening breeze on my
bottom already," said Nettle.

"Stop worrying," said Brilliance.
"Dame Fuddle's going to love it."

"What is this all about, Lavender?"
asked Dame Fuddle, peering through
the flowerpot door. "Why are we— *oh!*"

"Was that a good 'oh' or a bad 'oh'?"

asked Ping as Dame Fuddle stared at the cornflower gown.

"Oh!" said Dame Fuddle again. She clasped her hands together. "It's magnificent! It's glorious!"

The Naughty Fairies crowded around
Dame Fuddle with relief as the Head
Teacher sank down into a chair and
gazed at the dress.

"This is what we've been trying to tell
you, Dame Fuddle!"

"We made it for you to wear at the
Fairy Fashion Show . . ."

"It's such a good colour for you . . ."

"The bodice is made of wolf-spider
silk so it's nice and stretchy if you've
eaten too many sugared buttercups . . ."

"Do you like the ants?"

"Try it on," said Brilliance eagerly.

Still looking dazed, Dame Fuddle
took the dress behind a leaf screen in
the corner of the classroom.

"On the subject of trying it on," Dame
Lacewing warned, "I—"

Dame Fuddle emerged shyly from
behind the screen, clutching the
pompom hem in her hands. Dame
Lacewing's voice dried up and stopped.

"It fits!" squeaked Tiptoe.

"Perfect!" squealed Sesame.

"With some great hair and a pair of bluebell slippers, it'll be brilliant," said Brilliance happily.

Dame Lacewing cleared her throat. "I'm impressed," she said.

The Naughty Fairies glowed with pride. They'd done something right, and it felt good.

Dame Lacewing glanced around the rest of the Fairytailoring classroom.

Dresses and accessories were scattered over every surface. Wanda the wax fairy was wearing so many layers of petals that she looked like a football. The exhausted money spiders had fallen asleep in one corner, and Dollop was lying on his back in his cage with his mouth open.

"Lord Gallivant really has achieved

something here," said Dame Lacewing in
amazement. She glanced at Dollop.
"Though what a maggot is doing in a
Fairytailoring classroom, I can't imagine."

"It's a silkworm, Dame Lacewing,"
said Sesame. "Lord Gallivant bought it
from an imp. It cost him a lot of money
he said."

"No," said Dame Lacewing kindly.
"It's a maggot."

The evening air was calm and still.
Fireflies lit the entrance to the Wood
Stump, and the Stump's vast wooden
hall was polished to the colour of dark
honey. At both ends of the hall hung
long moss-green curtains, hiding the
backstage activity of St Juniper's and
Ambrosia Academy from the audience.
Two glittering catwalks snaked away
from each set of curtains, and met in
the centre of the Wood Stump in front of
a large crystal throne.

The Naughty Fairies peered through
the curtains at the assembled audience
of fairies, pixies, imps and gnomes.

"The catwalks are made of ice," said
Brilliance in excitement. "On the Fairy
Queen's orders! Ice shows off the
clothes to their best advantage,
according to Lord Gallivant."

"What happens if you fall over?" Sesame asked.

"The Fairy Queen sees your pants," Tiptoe said.

"On the subject of pants," said Nettle, "Dame Fuddle's bloomers don't fit as well as I'd like, but they'll have to do. Kelpie did her hair. It's great."

"Flea was my inspiration," said Kelpie, stroking her bumblebee.

"Lord Gallivant couldn't believe his

eyes," said Ping with a grin.

There was a fanfare. Everyone in the Wood Stump looked at the door.

The Fairy Queen had entered the hall with four elf attendants. She was so beautiful that it was like looking at the sun. Her blonde hair gleamed on top of her head and she wore a gold and purple bee-orchid dress which matched her golden wings. Her shoes shimmered with tiny crystals, and her crown sparkled with dancing dewdrops.

A nervous-looking Ambrosia Academy fairy with a blonde halo of curls stood up. "Welcome, Your Majesty, on behalf of Ambrosia Academy," she squeaked, smoothing down her pink rose-petal uniform. "May the clouds part at your coming and the stars glint at all your jokes."

There was a respectful cheer from behind the curtain at Ambrosia Academy's end of the room. The fairies

of St Juniper's muttered darkly under their breaths.

"We thank you for your good wishes," said the Fairy Queen in a tinkling bell-like voice.

"Ooh!" said Ping, putting her eye to the curtain. "Pelly's doing our welcome speech, look!"

A blonde fairy with pompom bunches over both ears stood up, scratched herself and stared at the ceiling. "Good to have you, Your Royalty, on behalf of St Juniper's," she said. "Um – that's it."

"St Juniper's rocks!" roared Brilliance, making the other fairies behind the St Juniper's curtain leap out of their skins.

The Fairy Queen nodded graciously. She sat down in the crystal throne and rested her fine white hands in her lap. Then suddenly, her hands were holding a slim piece of crystal as delicate as a frosted snowflake.

"The Fashion Feather," murmured
Nettle in awe.

"It's beautiful!" Tiptoe gasped.

"I want it in our dormitory when we
win it," said Brilliance.

"Don't you mean 'if'?" Sesame asked.

"I *never* mean 'if'," Brilliance said.

"To your places!" called Lord
Gallivant grumpily.

"Poor Lord Gallivant's heard so many
maggot jokes that he's in an awful
temper," Ping said.

"Talking of maggot jokes," said Nettle, "have you heard the one about—"

"To your place, Nettle!" shouted Lord Gallivant. "Doesn't anyone realise how serious this is?"

There was a roll of drums. The moss curtains at both ends of the hall swung back and the Fairy Fashion Show began.

Each school had entered five designs for the Fashion Feather: winter wear, daywear, summer wear, flywear and, last of all, evening wear.

Ambrosia Academy's winter wear design made the room gasp. A beautiful fairy with wavy hair swayed out in a dress made of fire, which flickered around her slim ankles as she glided down the catwalk.

"A dress of flames would certainly keep you warm in winter," said Brilliance honestly.

"But what if you set fire to your wings?" Ping asked.

The Fairy Queen leaned forward intently, then whispered something to an elf attendant by her side.

"The Queen likes it," Kelpie muttered stroking Flea rather hard.

"Onion's dress is just as good," said Tiptoe loyally.

A thin fairy with green hair and an even greener face tottered on to the St Juniper's end of the catwalk in a long nettle gown, a thickly knitted moss coat and very high rose-thorn slippers.

"Rub your slippers in the sandbox before you go out, Onion!" shouted Lord Gallivant.

"Too late," groaned Ping, as Onion slipped on the ice and landed flat on her face. It wasn't a good start.

Daywear was next. Ambrosia Academy's outfit looked as if it had been made from hundreds of tiny starflowers.

"The starflowers are shining like real stars – look!" Brilliance said.

"They won't show in the daylight," said Sesame.

"A waste of magic," Tiptoe agreed.

The Fairy Queen whispered again to her attendants as the second St Juniper's model clambered on to the catwalk. It was Onion's sister Vetch, wearing the snowdrop miniskirt with a bright pink fuchsia top and a fuschia-petal scarf tied around her pink head. The Fairy Queen smiled in approval.

"It's going to be close," whispered Ping in excitement as the summer-wear outfits – a transparent cobweb kaftan

from Ambrosia Academy
and a little jasmine
bikini from St
Juniper's – both
earned a nod
from the Fairy
Queen.

The flywear
category didn't
need the catwalk.
Glitter's friend Gloss shot from behind
the Ambrosia Academy curtain in a
whirl of daisies, her wings edged with
sparkling fairy dust. The room
applauded.

"Go, Marigold!" cheered the Naughty
Fairies as a brown-haired fairy flew out
in an eye-catching dress made of
fluttering red, gold and brown leaves.

As Marigold flitted around the room,
Glitter's head popped out from behind
the Ambrosia Academy curtain.
Catching Brilliance's eye, Glitter made

a cutting motion across her
throat, grinned slyly and
disappeared
again.

"Is it me, or is
it cold in here?"
Sesame said.

Lord Gallivant
appeared. He
seemed more cheerful. "Time to fetch
Dame Fuddle," he told the Naughty
Fairies. "I must say, that wolf-spider silk
bodice does wonders for her figure.
Let's all cross our wings, eh? May the
best design win!"

From the far side of the room, Lady
Campion emerged from behind
Ambrosia Academy's curtains. The
room oohed in approval at her evening
gown: a column of pure white lily with
a delicately woven grass rosette sitting
on one shoulder.

"Oh," groaned Sesame. "It's gorgeous!

So elegant, and classic, and . . ."

" . . . dull as dung," said Kelpie.
"Come on! Our turn next!"

"You look fantastic, Dame Fuddle,"
Nettle promised, as the Naughty Fairies
led their rather pale-looking head
teacher towards the curtain.

"Are you quite sure about the hair?"

asked Dame Fuddle weakly, patting the blue and white striped chignon on the top of her head.

"Go!" hissed Brilliance, giving Dame Fuddle a gentle push.

Dame Fuddle rubbed the tips of her bluebell slippers in the sandbox, scooped up the fluffy pompom hem on the cornflower gown and stepped on to the catwalk.

Lady Campion was still standing beside the Fairy Queen as Dame Fuddle moved carefully down the ice runway. She skidded briefly, but recovered and marched on, holding her head a little higher as she reached the Fairy Queen's throne.

"She's made it!" beamed Nettle. "For a minute there . . ."

With a slithery noise, Dame Fuddle's jasmine bloomers fell down. Lady Campion smirked. Politely, the Fairy Queen averted her eyes as Dame

Fuddle hauled her bloomers up again.

"It's over," said Tiptoe in despair.

Standing up, the Fairy Queen summoned all the models to stand around her on the ice catwalk.

"We have reached our decision," she said. "The standards have been high, but we feel that—"

There was a crackling sound as the pompoms around Dame Fuddle's hem

suddenly exploded.
To everyone's
astonishment,
hundreds of tiny
spiderlings hurtled
into the air.

"The pompoms!"
Nettle squeaked.

"They aren't
pompoms at all,"

Kelpie said.

"They're *wolf-spider
eggs!*" Sesame gasped.

More pompoms exploded
in a shower of
spiderlings. The spider babies
scampered down Dame
Fuddle's dress and raced off

in a hundred different
directions. Cheers erupted
around the hall as one of
the Ambrosia Academy
models screamed and ran,

forgetting about the icy catwalk and sliding off into the audience.

Then a large, eight-legged shadow loomed at the door of the Wood Stump, and the mother wolf spider trotted into the hall. Tumbling over each other, the spiderlings raced to their mother and jumped on to her back with squeaks of delight. The ice catwalks creaked and splintered as fairies and pixies and gnomes and imps fled from the hall, pushing and shoving and shouting with terror.

"Dame Lacewing's coming!" gasped Sesame.

Like an avenging black cloud, Dame Lacewing was heading straight towards the Naughty Fairies.

"Keep calm," Brilliance instructed, backing away from the curtain at speed. "This wasn't our fault."

"BRILIANCE!" a purple-faced Dame Lacewing bellowed.

"I don't think Dame Lacewing's going to believe us," Ping said.

"Plan B," Brilliance said. "RUN!"

7

An Ill Wind

"Just what I always wanted to do first thing in the morning," Kelpie grumbled. "Carry the world's fattest, most expensive maggot down three flights of stairs, across the courtyard and round to Turnip's maggot pen."

Dollop scratched himself on the bars as the Naughty Fairies puffed and heaved and lifted his cage on to their shoulders. They were on detention once again.

"I told you Dame Lacewing wouldn't believe us about the pompoms," Ping said with a sigh.

"It's not fair," Tiptoe grumbled. "We really tried to do something good for the school and we STILL got into trouble."

"I'm never being good again," Nettle said fiercely.

"I'm never good anyway," Kelpie said, shifting Dollop's cage to a more comfortable spot on her shoulder.

"Look on the bright side," said Brilliance. "St Juniper's hasn't officially lost the Fashion Feather yet."

"The Fairy Queen's making a decision this morning," Tiptoe said. "It'll probably come by pixie post today."

There was a gust of smelly wind.

"Pooh," Ping complained. "Is Turnip cooking cabbages, or did Dollop just fart?"

"What do you think?" Kelpie asked. "The sooner we get this stinking maggot round to the maggot pen, the better."

"I wonder if Lord Gallivant will ever see that imp again?" asked Nettle.

"Probably not," said Brilliance.

The Naughty Fairies heaved Dollop's cage into the courtyard and put it down for a moment.

"Excuse me?"

A grand-looking elf in a primrose tunic and a jaunty forget-me-not cap was standing underneath the dandelion clock and looking lost.

"Where might I find Dame Fuddle?" asked the elf.

The Naughty Fairies couldn't take their eyes off the large petal envelope in the elf's hands.

"She's busy," said Brilliance.

"We'll take the letter to her," Nettle offered, holding out her hand.

"I'm supposed to deliver it to Dame Fuddle in person," said the elf.

"We won't tell if you don't," said Kelpie with a wink.

There was another gust of cabbage-scented wind.

"Take it," said the elf, looking at
Dollop with disgust. He thrust the
envelope into Nettle's hand and hurried
away rather fast.

"Looks like maggots have their uses,"
said Tiptoe.

The Naughty Fairies studied the
envelope. The address had been written
in glittery golden ink, and bore the
stamp of the Royal Palace. After
checking for teachers, Brilliance
carefully peeled it open.

"What does it say?" Kelpie demanded.

"Have we lost?" asked Sesame.

"The Wood Stump is calling," Ping
said, biting her nails.

"We send greetings from the Royal
Palace," Brilliance read. "We greatly
enjoyed a most unusual evening at the
Wood Stump and commend you for the
originality of your designs, particularly
in the final category."

The others cheered.

We look forward to similar events in the future." Brilliance stopped and frowned. "Then the Queen signs her name. Look."

The Naughty Fairies peered at the elegant swirl at the bottom of the letter.

"Did we win or not?" Tiptoe asked.

"I don't know," said Brilliance. "It doesn't say."

A burst of sparkling snowflakes suddenly spilt from the envelope. They glittered in the air, and then – somehow – Brilliance was holding a slim piece of crystal, carved into the shape of a perfect feather.

"Are you going to tell Glitter, Brilliance?" Kelpie grinned, as the others screamed and whirled around the dandelion clock in a dance of delight. "Or can I? Oh please, can I?"

Also available from
Hodder Children's Books

Tricksy Pixie

The Naughty Fairies face a
challenge – to play the best trick on
Bindweed the garden pixie. Their
prank is SO good that Bindweed
quits St Juniper's. Who will look
after the school grounds now?

The Naughty Fairies of course!